Dear Parent:
Your child's love of reading starts here!

Every child learns to read in a different way and at his or her own speed. Some go back and forth between reading levels and read favorite books again and again. Others read through each level in order. You can help your young reader improve and become more confident by encouraging his or her own interests and abilities. From books your child reads with you to the first books he or she reads alone, there are I Can Read Books for every stage of reading:

SHARED READING
Basic language, word repetition, and whimsical illustrations, ideal for sharing with your emergent reader

BEGINNING READING
Short sentences, familiar words, and simple concepts for children eager to read on their own

READING WITH HELP
Engaging stories, longer sentences, and language play for developing readers

READING ALONE
Complex plots, challenging vocabulary, and high-interest topics for the independent reader

I Can Read Books have introduced children to the joy of reading since 1957. Featuring award-winning authors and illustrators and a fabulous cast of beloved characters, I Can Read Books set the standard for beginning readers.

A lifetime of discovery begins with the magical words "I Can Read!"

Visit www.icanread.com for information
on enriching your child's reading experience.

For the lovely Lynne,
who always gets *the pictures*
—H. P.

For Jane, Rosie, Chloe,
and Bunny, with love!
—L. A.

Gouache and black pencil were used to prepare the full-color art.

I Can Read Book® is a trademark of HarperCollins Publishers.
Amelia Bedelia is a registered trademark of Peppermint Partners, LLC.

Library of Congress Control Number: 2019937080
ISBN 978-0-06-293525-0 (hardback)—ISBN 978-0-06-293524-3 (pbk. ed.)

19 20 21 22 23 SCP 10 9 8 7 6 5 4 3 2 1 ❖ First Edition
Greenwillow Books

I Can Read!

BEGINNING 1 READING

Amelia Bedelia
·Gets the Picture·

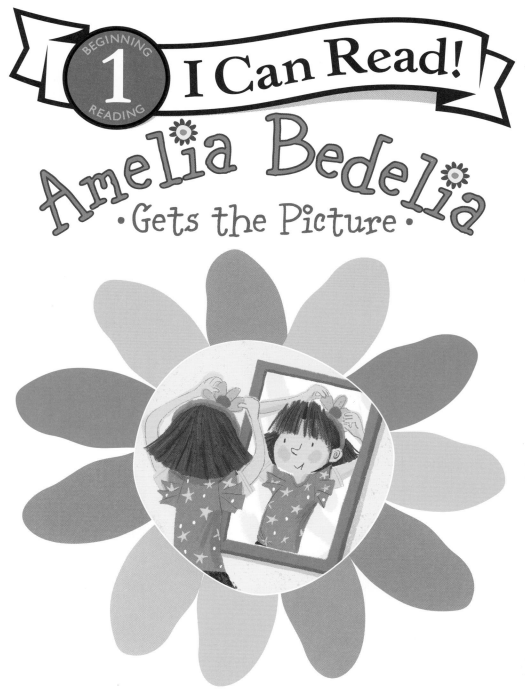

by Herman Parish ❀ pictures by Lynne Avril

Greenwillow Books, *An Imprint of* HarperCollins*Publishers*

Amelia Bedelia was in a hurry.

She did not want to miss

Picture Day.

"Don't you look nice," said Mr. Rice.

"I don't?" said Amelia Bedelia.

Amelia Bedelia looked in the mirror.

She checked herself.

Hair combed, check.

Clothes neat and clean, check.

Shoes matching, double check.

"I do not look nice," said Amelia Bedelia.

"I look amazing!"

Amelia Bedelia's classmates were
ready for Picture Day, too.

"I love your dress," Amelia Bedelia said
to her friend Dawn.

"Thank you," said Dawn.

"I was a flower girl in my aunt's wedding."

Some of the boys
wore jackets
and ties.

Everyone had their

hair combed,

even the new boy
in their class.

"Excuse me," said Amelia Bedelia

to the new boy.

"You are sitting in Clay's seat."

"I am Clay!" the boy said.

He stood up to prove it.

"Your bottom half is Clay
but your top half looks new,"
said Amelia Bedelia.

"This is my Picture Day plan," said Clay.

"I need to look good from the waist up."

"What about our class picture?"

said Amelia Bedelia.

"I always stand in the back," said Clay.

Rose struck a pose.
"Let's pretend
we are fashion models,"
she said.

"I am a model plane!"
said Angel.

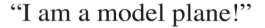

"ZZZZZZZOOOOOMMMMM!!!"

"Vroom VRRRRROOM!
I'm a model car,"
said Teddy.

14

"Let's be model students,"

said Miss Edwards.

"Please quiet down and pay attention."

Just then, a voice came
over the loudspeaker.

"I have bad news," said Mr. Rice.

"We are in a pickle.

The photographer has the flu.

Picture Day is canceled."

"Awwwww!" said the whole class.

Everyone was sad.

Everyone except Clay.

"Yippee! Hooray! Whoopee!" yelled Clay.

"I do not like Picture Day.

Dressing up is not the real me."

"I like pictures," said Amelia Bedelia.

"They help me remember my friends
and family."

"No photographer, no photos," said Wade.

"Let's get out of this pickle,"

said Amelia Bedelia.

"Let's draw our own pictures."

Amelia Bedelia got a piece of paper.

She got some colored pencils.

She got the mirror from the hallway.

"What is Amelia Bedelia doing?"

said Wade.

"Drawing a picture of herself,"

said Dawn.

"Why?" said Teddy.

"Does she have to draw

you a picture?" said Rose.

"Hey, I get the picture," said Clay.

"Amelia Bedelia is saving Picture Day."

The whole class drew
pictures of themselves.
"When I am famous, my picture
will be worth a lot of money," said Rose.
"Your picture is already worth
a thousand words," said Wade.
"Thank you!" said Rose.

25

"Let's play a game," said Miss Edwards.
She collected the pictures
and pinned them on the board.

Miss Edwards pointed at

a picture of a mountain.

"Who is this?" she asked.

"Cliff!" said the class.

"Who painted
this rosy picture?"
said Miss Edwards.
"Rose!" said the class.

"That's Dawn,"
said Holly.

"Penny!"
said the class.

29

Amelia Bedelia and her friends

were making so much noise

that Mr. Rice stopped by.

He admired each drawing.

"Don't you all look nice," he said.

"Who needs a camera?"

"Not me!" said Amelia Bedelia.

"Amelia Bedelia," said Mr. Rice.

"That is a good likeness of you."

"Thank you," said Amelia Bedelia.

Amelia Bedelia's picture

really was a good likeness.

She liked looking like a daisy.

She liked feeling happy.

She liked her friends most of all.

"Hooray for Amelia Bedelia," said Clay.

"This is our best Picture Day ever."